# PREHISTORIC LIFE

# Mammals, Birds and other Vertebrates

### BY CLARE HIBBERT AND RUDOLF FARKAS

**FRANKLIN WATTS**
LONDON·SYDNEY

Franklin Watts
This paperback edition published in Great Britain in 2023 by Hodder & Stoughton
Copyright © Hodder & Stoughton, 2023

All rights reserved.

Credits
Series Editor: Amy Pimperton
Series Designer: Peter Scoulding
Picture Researcher: Diana Morris

Picture credits:
Beatrissa/Shutterstock: 6.
Houston Museum of Natural Science, Houston, Texas. Daderot/CC Wikimedia Commons: 4.
Maija Karala/CC Wikimedia Commons: 5.
Mopic/Shutterstock: 7.

Every attempt has been made to clear copyright.
Should there be any inadvertent omission please apply to the publisher for rectification.

HB ISBN    978 1 4451 5888 4
PB ISBN    978 1 4451 5889 1

Printed in China

Franklin Watts
An imprint of
Hachette Children's Group
Part of Hodder & Stoughton
Carmelite House
50 Victoria Embankment
London EC4Y 0DZ

An Hachette UK Company
www.hachettechildrens.co.uk

Note to parents and teachers: Every effort has been made by the Publishers to ensure that the websites in this book are suitable for children, that they are of the highest educational value, and that they contain no inappropriate or offensive material. However, because of the nature of the Internet, it is impossible to guarantee that the contents of these sites will not be altered. We strongly advise that Internet access is supervised by a responsible adult.

# CONTENTS

| | |
|---|---|
| 4 | The First Animals |
| 6 | Endings and Beginnings |
| 8 | Dimetrodon |
| 10 | Temnodontosaurus |
| 12 | Pteranodon |
| 14 | Elasmosaurus |
| 16 | Mosasaurus |
| 18 | Megalodon |
| 20 | Phorusrhacos |
| 22 | Megatherium |
| 24 | Smilodon |
| 26 | Woolly mammoth |
| 28 | Timeline |
| 30 | Glossary |
| 31 | Further information |
| 32 | Index |

# The First Animals

Dinosaurs are the best-known prehistoric beasts. However, countless other animal groups appeared – and died out – in the billions of years before humans appeared on Earth.

## Fossil Evidence

Fossils are the preserved remains of animals that, over millions of years, have been turned into rock. Each new fossil discovery tells us more about the animals of the past.

▽ The study of fossils is called palaeontology. This fossilised skeleton is an Archegosaurus, a salamander-like animal that lived 299–253 million years ago (mya).

## From sea to land

Animals are organisms made up of many cells and are able to move, eat and reproduce. The first animals were invertebrates, or animals without backbones. Even today, around 97 per cent of all animal species on Earth are invertebrates – they include insects, spiders, crabs, snails and starfish. This book is about vertebrate animals – ones with backbones. Only 3 per cent of animal species are vertebrates.

Fish, the first vertebrates, appeared in the ocean around 500 mya.* About 100 million years later, four-legged fish crawled out of the ocean and on to land. They were the ancestors of all land vertebrates, including birds and mammals.

*All the dates in this book are approximate.

FROM SEA TO LAND
500–400 mya

400 million years ago

500 million years ago

- *Pederpes*
- *Ichthyostega*
- *Acanthostega*
- *Tiktaalik*
- *Panderichthys*
- *Eusthenopteron*

# Endings and Beginnings

There have been five major extinctions on Earth since life began. Each time, at least half the animal species were wiped out. Each time, new species have evolved to take their place.

## Periods of time

The history of life on Earth is mind-boggling. Geologists break it into smaller chunks called periods. They identify each period by looking at the rocks that formed at that time. The first mammal fossils appear in rocks from the Cretaceous Period. Woolly mammoths, which lived at the same time as early people, were around in the Quaternary Period, which is still going on.

## Myths and Stories

Before modern science, fossilised jaws and other bones must have been puzzling and even frightening. Perhaps they inspired people to make up stories about monsters, dragons and other mythical beasts.

< *Complete skeletons of prehistoric animals are very rare. This mammoth skeleton is about 80 per cent fossilised bone. The remaining 20 per cent is made of resin.*

Animals appeared in the Cambrian Period. The big stretch of time from when Earth formed until the start of the Cambrian Period is called the Precambrian Eon, which occurred 4,600–541 mya.

| Period | Million years ago | Major extinction event |
|---|---|---|
| Cambrian | 541–485 | |
| Ordovician | 485–443 | |
| | | First: 455–430 mya |
| Silurian | 443–419 | |
| Devonian | 419–359 | |
| | | Second: 407–359 mya |
| Carboniferous | 359–299 | |
| | | Third: 266–252 mya |
| Permian | 299–252 | |
| Triassic | 252–201 | |
| | | Fourth: 201 mya |
| Jurassic | 201–145 | |
| Cretaceous | 145–66 | |
| | | Fifth: 66 mya |
| Palaeogene | 66–23 | |
| Neogene | 23–2.6 | |
| Quaternary | 2.6–Today | |

*An asteroid hitting Earth probably caused the big extinction at the end of the Cretaceous Period. It threw up enough dust to block out sunlight for decades.*

# DIMETRODON

**PRONUNCIATION:** die-MEET-ruh-don
**GROUP:** Synapsids
**LIVED:** Permian Period, 295–272 mya
**RANGE:** Europe, North America
**HABITAT:** Dry scrubland, wetland
**WEIGHT:** 250 kg (550 lb)
**LENGTH:** 3.5 m (11 ft)

The fearsome predator *Dimetrodon* lived more than 40 million years before the first dinosaurs and was bigger than a family car. It ate fish, amphibians and reptiles.

*Dimetrodon* had an enormous sail on its back, which was supported by rods that branched out from its spine. The sail gave the animal's body more surface area, so it could heat up quickly in the morning when it basked in the sun. Like today's reptiles, *Dimetrodon* was not able to make its own body heat. *Dimetrodon* might have also used its sail to threaten attackers or impress a mate.

## TOOTH TYPES

*Dimetrodon* was a carnivore, and its short snout was packed with more than 80 teeth – sharp canines at the front and broader teeth at the back for grinding up muscle and bone. The name *Dimetrodon* means 'two measures of teeth'.

Dimetrodon's legs splayed out to the side like a lizard's – they weren't upright like a dinosaur's.

# TEMNODONTOSAURUS

**PRONUNCIATION:** tem-no-DONT-uh-SAWR-us
**CLASS:** Reptiles
**LIVED:** Early Jurassic Period, 200–175 mya
**RANGE:** Europe
**HABITAT:** Deep or open ocean
**WEIGHT:** 4.5 tonnes (5 tons)
**LENGTH:** 12 m (39 ft)

*Temnodontosaurus* was a gigantic ichthyosaur – one of the dolphin-shaped marine reptiles that lived in dinosaur times. In spite of their fishy appearance, ichthyosaurs could not breathe underwater and had to come up to the surface for air.

## LIVE BABIES

Most reptile babies hatch from eggs, but ichthyosaur mothers developed the eggs inside their bodies and then gave birth to live young. This is called being viviparous, and some snakes reproduce like that today.

Most ichthyosaurs were about 3 m (9.8 ft) long, but *Temnodontosaurus* was four times that! Its most striking feature was its dinner-plate-sized eyes, which were probably the largest eyes of any animal on Earth, ever. At 20 cm (8 in) across, they helped it to see in its gloomy, deep-ocean home. This predator slipped through Jurassic seas looking for squid, fish, plesiosaurs and other prey.

*Temnodontosaurus even hunted other ichthyosaurs, such as the much smaller Stenopterygius.*

# PTERANODON

**PRONUNCIATION:** ter-AN-oh-don
**CLASS:** Reptiles
**LIVED:** Late Cretaceous Period, 86–84.5 mya
**RANGE:** North America
**HABITAT:** Coastal areas
**WEIGHT:** 25 kg (55 lb)
**LENGTH:** 1.8 m (6 ft)

*Pteranodon* was a large pterosaur, one of the flying reptiles that swooped through the skies 215 to 66 mya. Over 1,200 *Pteranodon* fossils have been found – more than of any other pterosaur.

## BIRD-LIKE BEAK

*Pteranodon*'s name means 'wing without tooth'. Unlike earlier pterosaurs, it did not have any teeth. Its jaw was more like a bird's beak. *Pteranodon* must have gulped down fish whole, just like a pelican!

With a wingspan of 6 m (20 ft), *Pteranodon* was larger than any of today's seabirds, but it probably fed in a similar way. It could have flown low over the sea and snatched fish swimming near the surface. It was also the perfect, streamlined shape for diving head first into the water like a gannet, thanks to its long, sharp beak and backwards-pointing head crest. *Pteranodon* probably showed off its crest to attract a mate.

*Pteranodon's large wings made it an expert at gliding, but it could also flap its wings. Before the pterosaurs, only insects had managed to fly.*

# ELASMOSAURUS

| | |
|---|---|
| PRONUNCIATION: | ee-LAZ-moh-SAWR-us |
| CLASS: | Reptiles |
| LIVED: | Late Cretaceous Period, 80.5 mya |
| RANGE: | North America |
| HABITAT: | Open ocean |
| WEIGHT: | 2 tonnes (2.2 tons) |
| LENGTH: | 10.3 m (38 ft) |

Plesiosaurs were long-necked marine reptiles that lived at the same time as dinosaurs and pterosaurs. One group had particularly long necks. They are called elasmosaurs, and were named after *Elasmosaurus*, which was the first one to be discovered.

Like many marine hunters, *Elasmosaurus* probably had a dark back and a light belly. Its colouring would have helped it blend in with the seabed when viewed from above, and with the glimmering surface of the sea when viewed from underneath. A slow swimmer, it probably approached shoals of fish from below, then bobbed up its head to gulp down as many as it could before they all swam off.

### PAIN IN THE NECK?

*Elasmosaurus*'s long neck took up more than half its body length! It contained more than 70 neck bones - by comparison, a giraffe has only seven. No land animal could ever support a neck as long as *Elasmosaurus*'s.

*Elasmosaurus gulped down its catch without chewing. Stones in its gut helped to grind up its food.*

# MOSASAURUS

**PRONUNCIATION:** MOZ-uh-SAWR-us
**CLASS:** Reptiles
**LIVED:** Late Cretaceous Period, 70–66 mya
**RANGE:** Western Europe and North America
**HABITAT:** Oceans and shallow seas
**WEIGHT:** 5 tonnes (5.5 tons)
**HEIGHT:** 14.5 m (47.5 ft)

Mosasaurs are a group of reptiles that take their name from *Mosasaurus*, a ferocious marine predator that lived at the end of the Cretaceous Period. Mosasaurs hunted the same foods as ichthyosaurs and were so successful that their rivals became extinct!

*Mosasaurus* had a large head and a sleek but massive body. It hunted turtles, plesiosaurs, ichthyosaurs and smaller mosasaurs. Like modern snakes, it had a double-hinged jaw that allowed it to swallow prey whole. *Mosasaurus* waved its tail up and down to cruise through the water and steered with its flippers. This reptile could not support its body on land – instead, it gave birth to live young in the water.

## CUVIER'S CLUE

The first *Mosasaurus* fossil – a skull – was found just outside Maastricht (now in the Netherlands) in 1764. French scientist Georges Cuvier (1769-1832) mentioned the find as proof in his theory about cycles of extinction in the animal kingdom.

*Mosasaurus's long, narrow jaw contained 40–50 sharp, cone-shaped teeth.*

# MEGALODON

| | |
|---|---|
| PRONUNCIATION: | MEG-a-LOH-don |
| CLASS: | Cartilaginous fish |
| LIVED: | Neogene Period, 16–2.6 mya |
| RANGE: | Warm, coastal waters |
| HABITAT: | Worldwide |
| WEIGHT: | 73 tonnes (80 tons) |
| LENGTH: | 18 m (60 ft) |

Monstrous megalodon was one of the largest hunters to ever live on Earth. This outsize shark was three times the length of today's great white shark.

## THE STORY OF SHARKS

Sharks first appeared around **450** mya – long before the dinosaurs. They are one of our planet's oldest life forms. Today, there are more than **500** shark species swimming in the oceans.

Sharks belong to a group of fish that have skeletons made of cartilage instead of bone. Cartilage does not fossilise as easily as bone, so prehistoric sharks are known only from their teeth. Their body sizes are based on guesswork! Megalodon's teeth were more than 15 cm (6 in) long. Its jaws had a bite force of up to 18,600 kg (41,000 lb) – strong enough to crush a whale's skull.

*Megalodon consumed about a tonne of food every day! It hunted marine mammals, such as whales, dolphins and porpoises.*

# Phorusrhacos

**PRONUNCIATION:** FOE-roos-RAY-cuss
**CLASS:** Birds
**LIVED:** Early Neogene Period, 12 mya
**RANGE:** South America
**HABITAT:** Grassland
**WEIGHT:** 136 kg (300 lb)
**HEIGHT:** 2.4 m (8 ft)

Better known as the 'terror bird', *Phorusrhacos* was truly terrifying. It was slightly shorter than an ostrich, with a huge head and a massive, hooked beak for tearing into flesh.

Too heavy to fly, *Phorusrhacos* was able to hit speeds of 48 kph (30 mph) thanks to its long, muscular legs – although it was not as fast as an ostrich. Once it had chased down its mammal prey, the terror bird gripped it in its talons and tucked in with its beak. It might have thrown larger prey against a rock in order to stun it and break its bones.

## DINOSAUR DESCENDANTS

All birds, including the terror bird, evolved from dinosaurs. They survived the great extinction of 66 million years ago that wiped out other dinosaurs, pterosaurs and plesiosaurs.

*Almost two-thirds of the terror bird's huge skull was made up of its deadly, curved beak.*

# MEGATHERIUM

| | |
|---|---|
| **PRONUNCIATION:** | MEG-a-theer-EE-um |
| **CLASS:** | Mammals |
| **LIVED:** | Neogene Period to Quaternary Period, 5 mya – 11,000 years ago (ya) |
| **RANGE:** | South America |
| **HABITAT:** | Woodland, grassland |
| **WEIGHT:** | 4 tonnes (4.4 tons) |
| **LENGTH:** | 6 m (20 ft) |

Elephant-sized *Megatherium* was one of the largest land mammals ever. Also known as the giant ground sloth, its closest living relatives are anteaters, armadillos and tree sloths.

*Megatherium* was one of the enormous animals that evolved to fill the gap that was left behind when the dinosaurs died out. Others included giant beavers, wombats, deer, horses and rhinos. Like these, *Megatherium* was a herbivore. It could rear up to rip branches off trees with its massive, clawed 'hands'. Under its shaggy coat, bony plates called osteoderms helped to keep in body heat and protect it from predators.

## THE END

*Megatherium* became extinct around the end of the Ice Age, about **11,000** years ago. It probably could not cope with the warmer climate. It is also possible that this slow-moving giant was an easy target for human hunter-gatherers.

*Megatherium moved around on all-fours, but sometimes reared up to feed. Its tail helped it to balance.*

# SMILODON

| | |
|---|---|
| **PRONUNCIATION:** | *SMILE-oh-don* |
| **CLASS:** | Mammals |
| **LIVED:** | Quaternary Period, 2.5 mya – 10,000 ya |
| **RANGE:** | North and South America |
| **HABITAT:** | Woodland, grassland |
| **WEIGHT:** | 400 kg (880 lb) |
| **LENGTH:** | 2.25 m (7.4 ft) |

*Smilodon* was the biggest feline ever, as heavy as four jaguars! Its nickname, the 'sabre-toothed tiger', comes from its canine teeth – curved fangs that were up to 30 cm (12 in) long.

*Smilodon* was an apex predator. It hunted deer, buffalo, camels, ground sloths and even mammoths. Its hunting technique was to lie in wait in the low branches of a tree. When prey passed below, it leapt down and ambushed it, delivering a killer bite. *Smilodon* could open its jaws twice as wide as a lion can, but if it broke either of its canine teeth, they never grew back.

## PACK LIFE?

Some *Smilodon* fossils show signs of wounds that had time to heal. A solitary hunter with serious injuries would have died of starvation. It is possible that *Smilodon* lived in packs, like modern lions.

Smilodon's outsize fangs could stab and slash at prey, such as these bison.

# WOOLLY MAMMOTH

**CLASS:** Mammals
**LIVED:** Quaternary Period, 400,000–10,000 ya
**RANGE:** Eurasia, North America
**HABITAT:** Grasslands
**WEIGHT:** up to 6 tonnes (6.6 tons)
**HEIGHT:** 3.5 m (11.5 ft) (at shoulder)

Mammoths were huge, hairy members of the elephant family. They lived on the grasslands of Europe, Asia and the Americas until just after the last Ice Age.

Unlike modern elephants, which have evolved large, flappable ears to stay cool, mammoths had small ears that didn't lose body heat. Other adaptations for life in a cold climate included a thick, shaggy coat and big, bulky body. The fatty hump behind the mammoth's head stored energy, just like a camel's hump, so the animal could survive in the coldest months when food was scarce.

## TERRIFIC TUSKS

Mammoths' long, curved tusks kept growing throughout their life. They were good defence against attackers, such as sabre-toothed tigers. They could also be used to clear away snow to get at plants underneath.

*Mammoths lived in family groups called herds, just like elephants today.*

# TIMELINE

This timeline shows the different periods, or chunks of time, since life began on Earth. It includes the appearance of key species in this book, as well as when some of them became extinct.*

Eon

**Precambrian 4,600–541 mya**
    3,600 mya      First life forms – bacteria
    640 mya      First animals (sponges) appear

Era    Period

**PALAEOZOIC 541–252 mya**

**Cambrian 541–485 mya**

**Ordovician 485–443 mya**
    455–430 mya      First major extinction wipes out 85 per cent of all species

**Silurian 443–419 mya**

**Devonian 419–359 mya**
    400 mya      Ammonites, flying insects and first land vertebrates appear
    407–359 mya      Second major extinction wipes out 75 per cent of animal species, including all land vertebrates

**Carboniferous 359–299 mya**
    354 mya      Land vertebrates evolve again

**Permian 299–252 mya**
    295–272 mya      *Dimetrodon*
    266–252 mya      Third major extinction wipes out 95 per cent of marine species and 70 per cent of land species

* All the dates on these pages are approximate.

Era    Period

## MESOZOIC 252–66 mya

**Triassic 252–201 mya**
- 250–215 mya — Dinosaurs, pterosaurs and plesiosaurs appear
- 201 mya — Fourth major extinction wipes out 76 per cent of all species

**Jurassic 201–145 mya**
- 200–175 mya — *Temnodontosaurus*

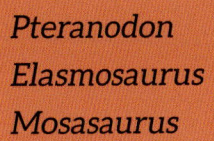

**Cretaceous 145–66 mya**
- 86–84.5 mya — *Pteranodon*
- 80.5 mya — *Elasmosaurus*
- 70–66 mya — *Mosasaurus*
- 66 mya — Fifth major extinction wipes out 80 per cent of animal species, including non-avian dinosaurs, pterosaurs, plesiosaurs and more

## CENOZOIC 66 mya–TODAY

**Palaeogene 66–23 mya**

**Neogene 23–2.6 mya**
- 16–2.6 mya — Megalodon
- 12 mya — *Phorusrhacos*
- 5 mya – 11,000 ya — *Megatherium*

**Quaternary 2.6 mya – today**
- 2.5 mya – 10,000 ya — *Smilodon*
- 400,000–10,000 ya — Woolly mammoth
- 200,000 ya — Our species, *Homo sapiens*, appears in Africa

# GLOSSARY

**amphibian** An animal with a bony skeleton and slimy skin that lives partly on land, partly in water, and cannot make its own body heat
**canine tooth** A long, sharp tooth found near the front of the mouth in carnivores
**carnivore** A meat-eater
**cartilage** Tough, flexible tissue attached to a bone, such as the tip of a human nose
**cell** The smallest part of a living thing that is able to function independently
**climate** The average weather of a place over a long period of time
**dinosaur** An extinct land reptile from the Triassic, Jurassic or Cretaceous periods whose legs came straight down from its body rather than splaying out like a modern reptile's
**evolve** To change from one species to another over millions of years, by passing on useful characteristics through the generations
**extinct** An animal or plant that has died out
**fossil** The remains of an animal or plant that died long ago, preserved in rock
**habitat** The natural home of a plant or animal
**herbivore** A plant-eater
**hunter-gatherer** Someone who lives by hunting, fishing and collecting wild foods
**Ice Age** The last time that the climate was so cold that huge ice sheets covered much of Earth, around 21,000 to 11,500 years ago.
**ichthyosaur** A dolphin-like, predatory marine reptile that lived in the Triassic, Jurassic and Cretaceous periods
**invertebrate** An animal without a backbone. Insects, spiders, worms, crabs and jellyfish are all invertebrates.
**mammal** An animal with a bony skeleton and fur or hair, and that can make its own body heat and feeds its babies on milk
**marine** Of or from the ocean
**osteoderm** The bony scales or plates usually found on a reptile's skin
**organism** A single living thing, such as a plant or an animal
**palaeontology** The branch of science concerned with the study of fossils
**plesiosaur** A long-necked, predatory marine reptile that lived in the Jurassic and Cretaceous periods
**predator** An animal that hunts other animals for food
**prehistoric** From the time before written records
**prey** An animal that is hunted by other animals for food
**pterosaur** A flying reptile with wings made from skin stretched over a long fourth finger
**reptile** An animal with a bony skeleton and scaly skin that cannot make its own body heat
**resin** A human-made material that is often used in making some plastics
**sabre-toothed** Describes an animal with long, curved canine teeth
**salamander** A small amphibian with a long, slender body and tail, and four short legs. Its skin often has brightly coloured markings.
**species** One particular type of living thing. Members of the same species look like each other and can reproduce together.
**synapsid** A primitive mammal
**vertebrate** An animal with a backbone. Fish, amphibians, reptiles and mammals (including humans) are all vertebrates.
**viviparous** Producing live young that developed inside the parent's body instead of laying eggs

# FURTHER INFORMATION

## Books:
*Birth of the Dinosaurs* by Michael Bright (Wayland, 2016)
*Children's Dinosaur and Prehistoric Animal Encyclopedia* by Douglas Palmer (QED, 2014)
*Dig Up a Mammoth* by Clare Hibbert (Arcturus, 2016)
*Dig Up a Sabre-Tooth Tiger* by Clare Hibbert (Arcturus, 2016)
*Dinosaur Infosaurus* series by Katie Woolley (Wayland, 2017)
*Graphic Prehistoric Animals* series by Gary Jeffrey (Franklin Watts, 2017)
*Prehistoric Mammals* by Professor Alan Turner (National Geographic Society, 2004)
*The Rise of Mammals* by Matthew Rake (Hungry Tomato, 2015)

## Websites:
www.bbc.com/earth/story/20150722-lost-beasts-of-the-ice-age
BBC guide to Ice Age creatures in Britain
www.nationalgeographic.com/animals/prehistoric
National Geographic Magazine's guide to prehistoric creatures
www.prehistoric-wildlife.com
An A-Z guide to prehistoric creatures
tarpits.org
The website of the La Brea Tar Pits and Museum in California, USA, home to many *Smilodon* fossils

## Places:
**The Dinosaur Museum**, Dorset
**Natural History Museum**, London
**National Museum**, Cardiff
**National Museum of Scotland**, Edinburgh
**Pitt-Rivers Museum**, Oxford
**Shropshire Hills Discovery Centre**, Craven Arms
**Ulster Museum**, Belfast

# INDEX

asteroids 7

beaks 12, 20
birds 5, 20–21

Cambrian Period 7
Carboniferous Period 7
Cretaceous Period 6–7, 12–17
Cuvier, Georges 16

Devonian Period 7
*Dimetrodon* 8–9

*Elasmosaurus* 14–15
extinctions, major 6–7, 16, 18–20

fish 5, 8, 10, 12, 15, 18–19

geological time periods 6–7

humans 6, 22

Ice Age 22, 26–27
ichthyosaurs 10–11, 16
invertebrates 5

Jurassic Period 7, 10–11

mammals 5–6, 19–20, 22–27
mammoth, woolly 6, 25–27
megalodon sharks 18–19
*Megatherium* 22–23
*Mosasaurus* 16–17

Neogene Period 7, 18–23

Ordovician Period 7
osteoderms 22

Palaeogene Period 7
Permian Period 7–9
*Phorusrhacos* 20–21
plesiosaurs 10, 14–16, 20
Precambrian Period 7
*Pteranodon* 12–13
pterosaurs 12–15, 20

Quaternary Period 6–7, 22–27

reptiles 8–17

sharks, megalodon 18–19
Silurian Period 7
*Smilodon* 24–25

teeth 8, 12, 16, 19, 25
*Temnodontosaurus* 10–11
Triassic Period 7